COVENANT OF THE ASHEN WOLF

VOL. 1

P. A. PEÑA

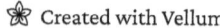 Created with Vellum

To my darling daughter, Liliana. While you may not be able to join me on this journey for quite some time, know that every step was taken for you.

CHAPTER 1

A WOLF FREED (KSARA POV)

The young girl's breath was heavy, and her lungs begged her to rest, if only for a few seconds. She couldn't. To do so would ensure a fate worse than death. Despite the fire burning in her legs and the aching of her bare feet as they slapped against the pavement, Ksara abided by two words echoing in her mind: *keep moving.*

Pedestrians filled the streets, each of them carrying on with their day. In a way, this worked in Ksara's favor. It would be harder to spot her among the crowds with more people around. But this also meant anyone who Ksara couldn't easily maneuver around quickly became acquainted with the sidewalk. She could hear the people around her talking, but the incessant beating of her heart drowned out their words. It was a stark contrast, her and the townsfolk. The monotony of their daily lives droned on as Ksara desperately clung to her first taste of freedom in five years.

Tattered rags hung off her body, barely held together by an equally frayed rope and exposing various parts of her sandy brown skin to the spring air. Despite this, Ksara was burning up as if she were in winter furs. Twenty minutes of nonstop running was beginning to take its toll. The back of her skull pulsed with a dull ache, and she felt lightheaded. Looking ahead, she spotted a dumpster in the alley across the street. Her heart felt as if it would burst from her chest at any moment, but the guards surely weren't that far behind. She shook her head and rounded the corner, knocking over another pedestrian. Ksara ignored the woman's cries and pressed onward. Soon she'd be at the town port and that much closer to securing her freedom.

Ksara stepped into the street. A horn blared, followed by the screech of rubber struggling to grip the asphalt. She turned her head to find a vehicle speeding toward her. In her haste to escape her pursuers, she hadn't noticed the oncoming traffic. The vehicle was small and compact, but it was still several times larger than she. Ksara had no time to move out of the way. She could do nothing but cringe, braced for the incoming impact.

As the vehicle struck her, jagged blue lines glowed upon her skin. The car wrapped around her body with a metallic crunch, as if it had hit a steel beam rather than a scrawny ten-year-old girl. Smoke billowed from under the folded hood, and glass scattered in the street. Ksara looked around. The car was totaled and the driver out cold. Or perhaps he was dead.

A crowd of people began forming around her.

"Somebody call the Saviors!" a man shouted as he tried to pull the driver's door open to no avail.

Ksara's eyes widened. If the Saviors found her, it would all be over. They'd turn her in for sure, and she wouldn't be able to keep the promise she had made to Serril.

"You little rat!" another man said, approaching Ksara, contempt burning in his eyes. Ksara winced as he took hold of her curly licorice-colored hair. "Look at all the damage you've caused!"

"Don't let her go!" a third man shouted.

Ksara's heart skipped a beat. She turned around as best she could. There they were, covered in armored plating and equipped with automatic rifles. The guards from the mine had caught up to her. In a matter of moments, they'd capture her. After the stunt she had pulled, she'd surely never see the light of day again. They'd keep her locked away, forcing her to mine gemstones for the rest of her life.

"No!" Ksara shouted. She concentrated all her effort into her arm. Her body began to glow with jagged red lines, and she pushed the man holding her.

The man flew back as if he had been blown away by a hurricane and collided with a shop window. Ksara took off once more, heading toward the town's port. If she could just make it there, she could stow away on a departing ship. She could hide among the cargo until she was far enough away from town. It was a slim chance, sure, but it was the only chance at freedom she had. She ducked into an alley and then into another. Even so, the guards were hot on her tail. She slipped into another alley only to come face to face with a chain-link fence about ten feet high.

"You have nowhere left to run," one of the guards shouted.

Ksara kept moving. She focused her energy, this time directing it into on her legs. Again, her body glowed with red lines and she leaped. Her foot hit the top of the fence, causing her to tumble over to the other side. She grunted, sucking in a breath as her face scraped against the ground. Wiping the blood from her cheek, she looked back. The guards split up, half of them running towards the fence and the others leaving the alley to head her off. Ksara pulled herself up and exited the alley. She gazed upon her destination just a few blocks away, a smile stretched across her face

The massive port was filled to the brim with people. Merchants' stands built from wood and cloth stood spaced about every ten feet or so. Many of them sold treasures from distant lands, but the food stands caught Ksara's attention the most. Their captivating smells drew her in like a moth to a flame. But of course, they would. It had been years since she had eaten anything beyond stale porridge and water. Ksara moved closer to a stand wafting the scent of honey, chiles, and garlic into the air. She pushed her way through the crowd of people until she was front and center. Her eyes widened at the sight of a woman tossing chicken breast in a bright orange sauce with a wooden spoon in a massive metal pan. Ksara licked her lips. Her stomach growled, and her mouth watered like a broken faucet.

"Excuse me," a man shouted, jolting her to attention. "Has anyone seen a young girl? Brown skin. Ragged clothes."

Slowly, Ksara eased back into the crowd and headed toward the ships. They were many and varied greatly in size and shape. Some were quite large and meant for transporting cargo, while others were smaller, specializing in speed and maneuverability. And, of course, there were the vessels that belonged to the Saviors. They were sizeable as well. However, they were not nearly as bulky as the cargo ships and carried canons as well as other weaponry.

Ksara approached a cargo ship on the far end of the port. Its hull was a dark black with metallic red trim. Its thrusters kept it hovering off the ground, and a large mast erected high into the sky. A pair of men loaded wooden crates onto the ship. One of them was tall and quite muscular. His skin was a tad darker than Ksara's, and his black hair was long and wavy. The other man was his opposite: short and pudgy, with pale white skin. He hadn't a hair upon his head, and he wore a pair of black oval sunglasses. Ksara ducked behind a corner and watched the men, waiting for her chance to approach.

As they grabbed another crate and began hauling it onto the ship, Ksara made her move. Carefully, she approached the remaining containers. Gripping the lid, she pried the box open. It contained sacks of rations and had just enough room for her to hide comfortably. Without a moment's hesitation, she entered the crate and placed the lid over her. It was pitch black, and the world outside was muffled through the wood. Ksara took a deep breath, trying her best to steady her nerves. Soon she'd be loaded onto the ship, and hopefully, not long after, they would have left town.

The crate shook as it lifted into the air.

"That's odd," a man said. His voice was high-pitched and a bit nasal.

"What is it?" a second man replied in a gruff and rugged tone.

"I don't know. Does this crate feel heavier to you?"

"It's the same as before."

The crate rocked back and forth.

"Don't do that," the second man said. "You're going to make me drop it."

"I swear this crate is heavier."

"It's fine. You're just getting tired, is all."

"You wish," the first man said with a scoff. "We should open the crate and make sure everything is all right."

Ksara covered her mouth and held her breath. Her body tensed as she prayed for the men to continue on.

"Can we please just finish loading the cargo?" the second man said, clearly irritated. "You know how upset Mirya will be if we don't get these loaded before she gets back."

The first man shuddered. "Good point."

The crate started moving again, and Ksara breathed a sigh of relief. Soon after, the box stopped with a thud. She was on the ship. All she had to do now was keep quiet and hide long enough for the boat to leave town. However, time seemed to be moving in slow motion, and the darkness only added to that feeling.

Outside of the crate, the crew of the cargo ship was conversing. Among the voices were the two men who loaded Ksara onto the ship along with a woman and a young boy. Their conversation was jovial as they discussed where their captain would be taking them next. The young boy wished to travel to the kingdom of Faelyn, while the woman confessed her desire to see Shyael. The men were in agreement, stating that they felt it was finally time for them to enter the inner realm of Mithrandir. The woman objected, noting that the boy, Draec, was far too young.

"Captain!" the crew said in unison.

"Not so loud," the captain replied. His voice was hoarse, making it even harder to hear him through the crate.

"Are you hungover again?" Draec said with a snicker. "You know Mirya isn't going to like that."

"What Mirya doesn't know won't hurt her."

"You say that every time you drink too much," the woman said, "and every time Mirya catches you."

"Don't be like that, Ovisia," the second man said. "After all, you drank just as much as us."

The first man let out a hearty laugh. "What do you mean? She drank us all under the table like she always does."

"Yes," Ovisia replied. "But I can hold my liquor."

Ksara was in shock. She didn't know what she'd expected of the cargo ship's crew, but she certainly hadn't expected this. They seemed close-knit and friendly, and yet reckless and rugged. It made her wonder just what cargo these people were transporting.

"Did you guys know that crate over there was opened?" the captain asked.

Ksara's heart dropped to her stomach. What was she going to do? She might as well be a fish in a barrel. She could hear the crew talking outside the crate, but she couldn't focus on what they said. She took a deep breath and tried to steady her nerves, but it was no use. All she could think about was the mines. How dank and dirty they were. The cramped living quarters and even tighter tunnels. Working past the point of exhaustion, only to wake up the next day and do it all over again. And now how would she survive without Serril by her side?

The lid lifted from the crate, and light pierced Ksara's eyes.

She squinted. All she could see was the silhouette of a man as she waited for her eyes to adjust.

"Well, well, well," the captain said as he reached into the crate and lifted Ksara into the air by her leg. "What do we have here?"

"I told you the crate was heavier," the short man said as he slugged the taller man in the arm.

"Oh, be quiet, Zeph," the taller man replied. "She's just a girl. A slave, by the looks of it."

The captain moved Ksara in front of his face and looked her in the eye. His were bloodshot, the red contrasting heavily with their icy blue irises. He had short chestnut brown hair that was shiny and full-bodied, and his skin was pale. A black hat with a white stripe reminiscent of a pirate's cap sat on his head, and he wore a red coat over a puffy white blouse.

"So," the captain said. "Just what are you doing on my ship?" His voice was stern, no longer carrying its previous carefree tone. Ksara was frozen. She didn't know what to say, and the longer the captain stared into her eyes, the tighter her throat seemed to get.

"Well?" the captain said. "I'm waiting."

Ksara swallowed the lump in her throat. "P-put me down," she said. "If you don't, you're going to regret it."

The man tightened his grip on Ksara's leg. "Threats are just words the weak use to try to exert control in this world. Those that are strong, the people meant to lead . . . they give orders." He pulled Ksara closer still, till their noses touched. "So, tell me. Which one are you?"

Ksara looked around. Everyone's eyes were on her, eagerly awaiting her answer. Blood rushed to her head, which only deepened her feelings of exposure. She took a deep breath. "Put me down," she said softly.

The captain turned to his crew. "Did that sound like an order to anyone?"

"Sounded more like a mouse whining for cheese," Zeph said with a chuckle. "What do you think, Nefion?"

"I don't know," he replied. "She sounded more like a cat to me."

Ksara couldn't help but frown. She balled her hands into fists and flared her nostrils.

"Okay," the captain said, turning back to face Ksara. "Why don't you—"

"Put me down now!" Ksara shouted as she cocked back her fist. Her body began to glow red just as it had before, and she struck the captain in his cheek.

Despite the force behind Ksara's punch, the captain didn't budge. A moment of silence passed before the cargo ship workers burst into boisterous laughter that came from deep in the gut.

"That's more like it," the captain said. He lowered Ksara to the ground. "You're all right, little wolf."

Ksara was confused, utterly so. On the one hand, the cargo ship captain seemed harsh and brutish. And yet, at the same time, he was kind and encouraging.

A group of men boarded the cargo ship, the sun casting bright reflections off their uniforms. Ksara gasped and took a step back.

"Finally," one of the guards said, stepping forward. "We have you now."

Zeph and Nefion stepped forward in turn, blocking his path and prompting the other guards to draw their weapons.

"That's mighty brazen of you, to board a ship uninvited," the captain said. "One might mistake it for a hostile action."

"You are harboring a fugitive on your ship," the guard said. "That girl is property of the Eladar Mining Company, and we are charged with returning her to her rightful owners."

Ksara tugged the captain's jacket causing him to look down at her. "Please," she said, nearly choking on her words as tears rolled down her cheeks. "Don't let them take me back."

The captain flashed Ksara a smile and took her hand, positioning her behind him. "I'm afraid you must be mistaken," he said as he turned his attention back to the guards. "You see, they call me Bandit Captain Elpys, and this ship is known as the *Horizon*. On this vessel, everyone is free."

The guards broke into cautious whispers. Some even took a few steps backward and slowly lowered their weapons.

"Listen," the guard up front said as he gestured to his men to calm down. "Either hand over the girl, or we'll open fire. You all are bandits harboring a fugitive slave. The law is on our side. I'm sure you don't want the Saviors to get involved."

Elpys burst out into laughter again—only this time, it carried a more sinister tone. He tightened his fists and began to walk toward the guards. However, he stopped when blood sprayed into the air and began to pool on the deck. The guard screamed in pain and dropped his rifle. It was so fast, Ksara hadn't even seen what happened, but Nefion now stood wiping the blood from his blade.

The guards trembled, looking as if they didn't know whether to run or empty their magazines.

"Consider yourself lucky you've only lost an arm," Elpys said. "Now get off my ship."

In a panic, the guards all left, dripping a trail of blood in their wake. As they ran off the ship, a tall, slender woman boarded. Her eyes were reddish-brown, and her hair was as dark as a raven's feather. It flowed in waves effortlessly and rested just above the small of her back. She wore a pair of blue jeans ripped at the knee, sandals, and a white tank top that stopped at her belly button.

"Mirya," Elpys said, rubbing the back of his neck. "You just missed the fun."

Mirya didn't respond but instead stared at him as if she were reading a book. "Fun? You think it's fun to draw attention to ourselves in every town we stop in? If you keep this up, there won't be anywhere we can dock safely. Do you not realize how hard you make my job, or do you just not care?"

"Of course I care," Elpys said. "But I can't help it if someone boards my ship and threatens my family."

Ovisia spoke up. "I hate to say it, but he's right."

Now that Ksara was out of the crate, she could see Ovisia. She was positively stunning. Her hair was a platinum blonde, and her white skin was moderately tanned. She wore a black tube top and fingerless gloves to match. Her boots had a slight heel, and her jeans were fitted, accentuating her curves.

Mirya scowled. "I sincerely doubt the only option was to cut off the man's arm."

"That was my fault." Nefion raised his hand. "I suppose I could have been more, uh, gentle, I guess."

"As if," Draec said. "That guy had about two more seconds before Elpys liquified him."

Ksara looked over at the young boy. He had remained silent during the confrontation, and Ksara had forgotten he was even there. He looked the same age as her but was obviously in better condition. He wore a pair of jean shorts and a vest to match. His hair was as white as snow, and he had intensely green eyes. As Ksara looked at Draec, she couldn't help but wonder why a boy his age would be traveling with bandits. He didn't look to be related to any of them, so just what was he doing here?

"Whatever," Mirya said. "I suppose what's done is done. I'll just have to add Eladar to the list of places we shouldn't go back to." She turned her attention to Ksara. "Who's the kid?"

"Hmm," Elpys said, stroking his chin. "You know, I forgot to ask."

"You forgot to ask..."

"Mm-hmm."

Mirya let out a heavy sigh as she pinched the bridge of her nose. "Why do I put up with you?"

"Because you're my vice-captain, and you *love* me."

"My name is Ksara Sepheron," she interjected. "It's a pleasure to meet you all."

The crew formally introduced themselves, then Elpys proceeded to walk towards the Horizon's interior. "I'm going to lie back down," he said. "Nobody bug me until dinner's ready."

"What are we supposed to do with the kid?" Mirya asked.

"That's up to her," Elpys replied with a wave. "If the little wolf is staying, get her some proper clothes and put her to work. We should probably get that blood cleaned up before it sets in."

As Ksara watched Elpys walk away, her vision became blurry. It faded more and more until he was gone.

She blinked, and she was no longer on the *Horizon*. She was in a cockpit, slumped over in her seat. Her lips were dry, and her throat even more so. Sweat drenched her brow, and her clothes were heavy and soggy.

"That's right," Ksara said faintly. "That was eight years ago."

She swallowed hard, then coughed. It felt like shards of glass dancing across her throat. Her eyelids were becoming heavy. Her breaths were slowing down, and darkness would be taking her soon.

"Elpys . . . I swear I'll see you again."

CHAPTER 2
A DIAMOND IN THE SAND (GERRIN POV)

There wasn't a cloud in the sky, which only intensified the already blistering early evening heat of the Hastos Desert. As usual, wildlife and vegetation were few and far between. As Gerrin barreled through the desert sands, his truck kicked up a thick cloud of dust in the wake of its four tires, thick gray smoke spouting from the tailpipe. It was a modest vehicle and quite dated. Parts of it were painted black, while others weren't painted at all. Gerrin had maintained it through years of scavenging parts from whatever sources were available. It was roofless, allowing a vigorous wind to tousle Gerrin's golden yellow locks. The arid wind did little to keep sweat from pooling on his skin, but at least it was something.

Every so often, Gerrin wiped the goggles shielding his eyes from the blowing sands. Like his truck, they too were past their prime. The left lens had been cracked in a minor accident back in his workshop, but other than that, they were still functional. Despite their ragged appearance, it never once crossed Gerrin's mind to replace them. He had far bigger priorities.

As Gerrin drove, one hand on the wheel and the other propping up his cheek, he caught a glimpse of his tired expression in the side mirror. It wasn't the tired look that came from a long restless night, although he had been awake for nearly sixteen hours. No, this was the kind of look that spawned from being completely and utterly stuck. Unable to move forward, yet equally incapable of going back to the way things once were.

Gerrin looked over at his passenger seat at the black box he'd picked up from Hastos. He didn't know what the contents of the package were. He never knew. More than a few times, he had considered opening the box, but that was years ago. His better judgment prevented him from doing so. Nowadays, Gerrin simply transported the boxes back and forth between Lasslail and Hastos, and convinced himself that he and his family would be better off with the boxes being a mystery.

Gerrin returned his eyes to the path in front of him, and his eyes widened with fright. A shape rose from the sand up ahead. It was impossible to make out what it was, but it was certainly large enough to total his vehicle. Placing both hands on the wheel, he swerved out of the way, managing just barely to miss the object. He slammed on the brakes and came to an abrupt stop. His heart was thumping in his chest, and his stomach churned in a tight knot. He took a deep breath and wiped the sweat from his brow before exiting his truck. Of course, he had a schedule to keep, and it was never a good idea to keep Nox waiting, but Gerrin's curiosity had always been a force he found difficult to subdue.

Whatever the object was, it was rather large. Bigger than Gerrin's truck, in fact. He brushed away some of the sand using his forearm, revealing metal plating. He continued unveiling more and more until it was apparent that the object in question was an abandoned vehicle. With a smile, Gerrin returned to his truck and pulled a small black disc from the glovebox. He stuck the disc to the metal on the abandoned vehicle and pressed its buttons in a practiced sequence. The abandoned vehicle began to glow a light blue. As it did, it rose out of the sand and levitated off the ground.

With the vehicle hoisted in the air, Gerrin could see it clearly now. It had no tires and instead used a trio of thrusters to maneuver. An elegant gunmetal gray paint job coated the vehicle, and a series of solar panels covered the roof. The windows were tinted too darkly to allow Gerrin to see what, if anything, was inside. He made a quick pass around the vehicle and failed to find a door of any kind. Luckily for him, there was a hitch that he could attach to the back of his truck. After securing the abandoned vehicle, he headed back to his village.

Lasslail was one of three villages located throughout the Hastos desert. It was the smallest of the three as well as the most remote. Sand dunes surrounded the area, and a sizable oasis rested in its center. The water was crystal clear, and the locals swore by its healing properties.

Legend had it that the oasis was once merely a puddle filled with muddy water until a woman of incomparable beauty stopped there. Needing to rest as she fled persecution, she dipped her weary feet into the water. Her radiance, overflowing in abundance, spilled into the puddle and purified it. The water magnified tenfold and grew to support Lasslail over the years. Gerrin's melon farm drew the resources needed to produce succulent fruit from the same source.

The village itself consisted of just over a hundred people, many of them either middle-aged or elderly. Gerrin, at nineteen, was the youngest adult. Under him were his twin sisters Lysabel and Eissa at fifteen, and under them were a handful of middle school children.

Gerrin's home rested just south of Lasslail, separating it from the desert. The Ruu family farm consisted of four melon fields, a large barn that doubled as Gerrin's workshop, and the house in which they dwelled. He pulled up to the gate, stopping as his grandmother, Olenor, approached his truck. Wrinkles covered nearly every inch of her white skin. She was tanned like Gerrin and wore a lilac-colored linen dress. A flower pin of the same color kept her gray hair tied up and out of her face.

"Gerrin," Olenor said, relief evident in her tone. "You're home."

Gerrin got out of his truck. "You sound as if I wasn't going to make it back."

He walked over to Olenor and gave her a firm yet gentle squeeze. She hugged him back, gripping him tightly as if he would float away if she didn't hold on with everything she had.

"Okay," Gerrin said with a cough. "I get it. I feel loved."

Olenor pushed Gerrin away in a flash and slapped him on the shoulder. "How many times are you going to do this?" she asked, planting her fists on her hips.

"We've already talked about this," Gerrin said as he took off his goggles.

He walked towards his truck and began unhitching the abandoned vehicle.

"Yes, and we'll keep talking about it until you stop this foolishness."

"I don't know what you want me to say."

"Say you'll quit."

Gerrin puffed out a breath of air. "It's not that simple. You don't just say no to Nox. Things might not be perfect, but they're better this way."

Olenor scoffed. Gerrin didn't need to see his grandmother to know that gesture included an eyeroll as well. "You think so."

"I know so." Gerrin stood up and turned around only to bump into his grandmother.

"They came to the farm this morning."

Gerrin tightened his fists, and his lips curled into a frown. "They what?"

"This morning, bandits came to the farm."

"Nox was here?"

Olenor chuckled. "A man like Nox doesn't get his own hands dirty. He sent two of his flunkies. The giant and the stupid one."

"Jabal and Aegar?"

"I don't know these people," Olenor said with a wave of her hand. "But they certainly know you. Just what have you gotten yourself into?"

"Gerrin!" Eissa shouted as she ran up to greet her brother. She was a tad lighter than he but shared the same hair and brown eyes, although her hair was much longer than his. Her sundress was a whirlwind of orange and white flower petals, and she wore a pair of brown sandals.

"Did the girls see them?" Gerrin whispered to Olenor.

Olenor shook her head. "They were busy tending to the melons."

"Don't mention a word of this."

"You know I won't," Olenor said. "But sooner or later, they're going to find out. They may be children, but they are not fools, Gerrin."

Eissa leaped into Gerrin's arms. For being so small, she had a fearsome grip. Gerrin smiled, but that smile quickly faded when he looked over to Olenor. Although she had turned away and looked towards the farm, he could still read the disappointment written all over her face.

"How was Hastos?" Eissa asked.

Gerrin gently pulled a golden curl away from her face. "The same as always."

Eissa giggled. "You always say that."

Gerrin stepped back and got into his truck. "It's always true."

He turned the key, and after a sputter, the engine began to rumble. "I gotta run into the village real quick."

Eissa frowned. "But you just got back."

"I know, I know. I just have some business to tend to in the village. I promise I'll be back before dinner."

Lasslail was uproarious, although the majority of the noise came from the saloon. As Gerrin rode through the sandstone brick buildings of the village, he could see his fellow villagers peering at him through their windows. Some bore expressions of hate, while others' faces held contempt. None of them bothered him in the slightest. After all, they paled in comparison to the piercing blades a mere glance from Olenor threw at him. He pressed onward, heading straight for the saloon.

The Respite had once been a pillar of the community. It served as a place to wind down after a long day working in the sun, but ever since Nox and his men had arrived in Lasslail, the business had seen better days. The front window was perpetually broken, and many cracks were present in the sandstone. Frankly, it was a miracle that it was still standing after years of neglect. Graffiti littered the eastern side of the building, and the front was always full of hoverbikes.

Gerrin parked his truck in front of the saloon. After grabbing the black box, he headed inside to find utter chaos. A man sat at the far end of the bar playing a piano. He was nervous, as evidenced by the stutters in his song and the keys he failed to hit. A pair of men sat at the table closest to him. For every mistake the pianist made, the men would toss an empty bottle at him, which obviously made the man more nervous. Thankfully the men were drunk off their asses and often hit the wall rather than the pianist.

The barkeep was hard at work preparing drink after drink as a slew of drunken men berated him for not moving fast enough. His two waitresses ran between tables and the bar, juggling glasses and plates of food, all while avoiding unwanted gropes.

A group of men played cards at one of the tables, and at another, men ogled a dancing woman. She was barely clothed, and her movements were sluggish and lacking rhythm. It was clear she was drunk as well, but the men sure didn't seem to mind. They howled like rabid dogs, begging the woman to take that final step into nudity.

Nox sat at the table furthest from the entrance with his back to the corner. He was a short man who wore his fiery red hair styled into a mohawk. His white skin was pale despite living in such a sun-drenched climate, and he wore nothing but a pair of black jeans and boots, revealing a lean, muscled frame.

On Nox's left stood Jabal. He was much taller, even more so than Gerrin. His skin was a deep dark brown, and he wore a pair of sunglasses despite being indoors. He was dressed in a pair of red denim pants and a vest to match. Most notable, though, were the two pistols holstered to his hips. They were a shiny silver with white wooden grips.

To Nox's right was Aegar. He was a blob of a man standing about as tall as Gerrin. A dark green tunic just barely covered his body, and he wore a pair of black tights that looked as if they would rip if he took a single step.

Gerrin and Nox locked eyes. Nox flashed a devilish grin, and Gerrin began walking over to him.

"It's good to see you," Nox exclaimed, leaning back in his chair. "I was beginning to get worried. I'm sure you already know by now I sent my best men looking for you."

Gerrin tossed the box, and it hit the table with a thud. The saloon quieted, and all eyes fell upon him. "We had a deal," Gerrin said. "I moved whatever the hell was in these boxes, and you bandits were never supposed to set foot on my family's farm."

For a moment, the saloon remained quiet. That is, until Nox burst into obnoxious laughter. The sound ignited every one of Gerrin's nerves. Nox glanced past Gerrin. He turned around to find a fist flying towards his face. He raised his arm, managing to block the incoming strike. Gerrin pulled his arm back and delivered an uppercut to his attacker. He took a defensive guard, preparing for a fight.

A bottle shattered across the back of Gerrin's head, and he yelped in pain as he slumped onto the floor. Two men grabbed Gerrin, lifted him, and pinned his face to Nox's table. The grip on the back of Gerrin's head was tight and entirely unnecessary. His vision was blurry, and the room looked as if it were swaying. He could feel his hair soaking with blood, but he couldn't focus his mind beyond the throbbing pain.

"I see I've been too lenient," Nox said. "I've allowed you to grow comfortable. To think you would come into my domain, my sanctuary, and be so disrespectful. It breaks my heart."

Nox reached over and grabbed the box. He opened it, revealing red cushioning and countless tiny vials shaped like hourglasses. Each was clear, showing a lime green liquid that swished with each movement. Nox grabbed a vial and held it just under his nose. He broke it in half, closed his eyes, and inhaled the green vapor that poured out from the broken vial. His eyes burst open, and his pupils dilated. Slowly, a green tint overtook the sclera of his eye. Wiping his nose, he leaned back in his chair once more.

"Tell me, Gerrin," Nox began, "Which one of your sisters do you like best?"

Nox's words lit a fire in Gerrin. He pushed against the hand holding him down, struggling to break free. A knife drove into the table, lodging deep into the wood mere inches from Gerrin's cheek. Gerrin's breaths were heavy, and it was clear he wasn't going anywhere. Even so, he stared Nox in his eyes as best he could.

"Listen up and listen good," Gerrin said, his voice stern and direct. "Touch my family, and I swear we'll all burn in hell together."

Again, the saloon fell silent only for the ice to be broken by Nox's insufferable laugh.

Nox stood to his feet. "Let him up," he said as he walked around the table.

The men pinning Gerrin to the table released him. The pressure on his head was gone, and as Gerrin stood, he rubbed his neck, hoping to alleviate the stiffness that set in. Nox stood just a few feet from Gerrin. He reached over and pulled the knife from the table. To Gerrin's surprise, he held out the handle, prompting him to take it.

"Go ahead," Nox said, prompting Gerrin to take the knife.

He paused, unsure of what Nox had in store.

Nox smiled. "Don't you get it?" He placed his hand on Gerrin's shoulder. "I'm giving you a chance here. You see, this knife represents your chance to make all of this go away. All you have to do is take it and drive it right here." He took the knife and placed the tip over his own heart. "It wouldn't take much effort at all. Just one swift motion and all your troubles would bleed out onto the floor."

As Gerrin looked into Nox's eyes, a chill ran throughout his body. His heart pounded like a piston in his chest, and the hairs on his neck stood straight up.

"Are you worried my gang would retaliate?" Nox asked. "I assure you they'd do no such thing." He turned to Jabal. "Isn't that right?"

Jabal nodded and spoke to Gerrin. "If Nox were to die to a pissant like you, I'd personally disband the gang."

"How about this? Let's make it even easier for you."

Nox slid the blade across his chest, carving an X into his flesh right over his heart. He didn't so much as flinch as blood trickled down his skin. He held out the blade's handle to Gerrin once more.

A grin twisted across Nox's face. "There. X marks the spot!"

Gerrin looked down at the blade, and his stomach began to knot. It was true. Killing Nox would solve all his problems. But could he really do it? Slowly he took the knife into his hand. It was heavier than he expected. Or perhaps it was the magnitude of the moment that weighed the knife down.

"Well?" Nox puffed his chest out. "We're all waiting."

Gerrin looked at Nox and the grin he loathed so much. All he had to do was push the knife through Nox's heart. It sounded so easy in his head, yet he couldn't bring himself to do it.

Until he thought of Olenor. The look in her eyes every time he hopped in his truck to ride away to Hastos. His sisters. Eissa and Lysabel. Nox had already broken their agreement once. How much longer would it be before he put his family in harm's way?

Gerrin tightened his grip on the knife and swallowed the lump in his throat. He cocked back and swung the blade with everything he could muster. But as the knife touched Nox's skin, the steel melted. Gerrin's eyes widened. The liquid metal drizzled down Nox's chest as if it were warm honey.

"And that represents your state in life," Nox said as he wiped the metal from his body. "You, along with everyone and everything in this village, belong to me. You are simply here because you are somewhat useful, but make no mistake. What you do for me can be done by anyone."

Gerrin stood frozen, completely and utterly in shock. Nox returned to his seat and placed his hand on Aegar's shoulder. With an oafish smile, Aegar walked over to Gerrin.

He knew he should run. Gerrin felt it deep in his bones. But no matter how hard his brain shouted at his body to move, he couldn't. Aegar swung his fist, punching Gerrin straight in his face. Gerrin flew back, knocking over a table and shattering glass everywhere. Aegar moved in and began kicking Gerrin as he writhed on the floor. With each kick, he grunted. His breath became labored and heavy as every blow forced the air from his lungs.

"One more thing," Nox said. "If you ever think about stepping out of line again, remember this beating and think of your family. Next time, your punishment falls on them."

CHAPTER 3
FROM BAD TO WORSE (GERRIN POV)

By the time Aegar finished working Gerrin over, the sun had begun its descent. The intolerable heat of the day was quickly becoming the insufferable cold of the night. Gerrin limped out of The Respite and headed over to his truck. Blood stained his clothes, and bruises covered his skin in various shades of blue and purple. A pulsating pain echoed in the back of his head. His bottom lip was split, and his left eye was swollen shut.

Despite being a battered mess, Gerrin didn't care about his injuries. He instead wondered just what he was going to say to his family when he got home. What would his sisters say when they saw their brother, their protector, beaten and run down? And Olenor. Disappointment was sure to be plastered all over her face. Gerrin teared up. He wiped his eyes, hissing in pain.

"It's not fair," Gerrin said, his voice hoarse. "It's just not fair."

He kicked the tire of his truck, only to lose his footing and collapse in the sand. He hunched over, tucking his knees into his chest as he wrapped his trembling arms around his legs. The tears flowed from his eyes like a mighty river. His body felt heavy, and he struggled to catch his breath.

"Mom. Dad. I don't know what to do. How am I supposed to keep everyone safe?"

Gerrin sat in the sand for a moment, unable to pull himself together. It wasn't until his stomach growled that he remembered the promise he had made to Eissa. Slowly, he pulled himself off the ground and got into his truck. The ride home wasn't nearly long enough.

The house spanned just one floor and a basement. It had but one bathroom and two bedrooms. Olenor slept in the master bedroom while the twins shared the other. That left the basement for Gerrin.

Gerrin walked up to the front door. He reached for the doorknob, pausing when his hand wrapped around the metal. He took a deep breath, twisted the knob, and pushed the door open. Olenor and the girls were in the dining room. He walked through the living room and stepped into the doorway. There they were, sitting down at a brown rectangular table. They had eaten without him, which was to be expected. He was late, after all. However, dinner was still on the table, and they sat there talking, waiting for him to get home. Tears began to fall from Gerrin's eyes once again as he looked at his family.

"Gerrin . . ." Lysabel said, shock evident in her face.

Physically, Lysabel looked exactly like her sister, only she cut her hair short and carried with her a boyish flair. She wore a pair of overalls and a white tee shirt underneath.

Eissa and Olenor turned around. Simultaneously they jumped out of their chairs and rushed over to Gerrin. Eissa made it first and wrapped her arms around her brother. He stumbled backward, wincing in pain as he hugged his sister back.

"Easy now," Gerrin said. "You squeeze me any tighter, and I'm afraid I might pop."

"I-I'm sorry," Eissa said as she pulled back. "What happened to you?"

Gerrin fell silent as he turned to Olenor. They traded glances, and Gerrin looked back to Eissa. She was an anxious mess, fidgeting in place as she waited for an answer. He opened his mouth to speak, but Lysabel beat him to it.

"It was Nox," she said as she stood up with an angry scowl.

Gerrin couldn't respond. He simply didn't know how. In all his time transporting drugs for Nox, he had tried so desperately to keep it from his sisters.

"Nox?" Eissa said with bewilderment in her tone. "Why would he want to hurt Gerrin?"

"Could you go and get the first aid kit for me?" Olenor said, turning to Lysabel. Lysabel didn't respond, but complied, nonetheless. Olenor then directed her attention to Eissa. "And do you mind getting me some clean towels?"

Eissa nodded. "Of course not."

Olenor pulled Gerrin over to the table and sat him down. She pulled up a chair next to him. They locked eyes, prompting Gerrin to turn away.

"I thought if I just did what he asked, he would leave you all alone," Gerrin said with a sniffle. "I told myself it didn't matter what I was doing, so long as you all were safe. It never bothered me that everyone in Lasslail looked down on me, and I was never afraid of being arrested. I would gladly lay down my life if it meant you guys would never have to deal with Nox."

"It was foolish to think a man like Nox would ever honor his word," Olenor said.

Her words, right as they were, cut right through Gerrin. Olenor reached over, placing her hand on his chin. Gently, she guided his face so that their gazes met again. Gerrin was in shock. Where he expected to see disappointment, he instead found warmth and compassion.

"You did what you believed was right," Olenor continued.

"That's what matters, and that is what I want you to hold in your heart."

Olenor smiled, and Gerrin couldn't help but return the gesture despite the sting it brought to his injured lip. As quickly as it came, Gerrin's smile faded, and he looked down at his hands.

"What is it?" Olenor asked.

"I don't want to do this anymore...but I don't know what else to do. If I tell Nox I won't work for him, he'll kill you and the girls."

"Then don't tell him."

Gerrin's brow raised in confusion. "What do you mean?" he asked.

Olenor placed her hand over Gerrin's. "For a while now, I've been gathering resources to move our family out of Lasslail. I don't quite have enough for us to leave and be comfortable, but I think it might be best to move up the timeline given recent developments."

"Leave Lasslail? But the farm—"

"Is not worth our lives. Don't get me wrong. This farm has been in our family for generations, and if I could, I'd rather stay here. But if I'm being forced to choose between watching my family be ripped apart by bandits or leaving my home behind, well, consider my bags packed."

The girls returned with the items Olenor had requested, and she began treating Gerrin's injuries. Olenor directed Gerrin to remove his shirt, uncovering even more cuts and bruises on his slim frame. After soaking a towel in warm water, Olenor cleaned the dried blood. He tried his best to keep still, but every so often, he winced as Olenor applied pressure to his injuries. With the blood cleaned off, she poured alcohol on a fresh towel and dabbed each of Gerrin's cuts. He sucked in a breath as the liquid burned his flesh. Finally, she placed bandages on each cut to ensure they were protected and could heal properly.

When they were done, Olenor fixed Gerrin a plate and

reheated it. The four of them sat down at the dinner table, and while Gerrin ate in painfully slow bites, his sisters told him about their day, although it was mostly Eissa who talked. Every so often, Lysabel added to the conversation when prompted, but she mostly sat silent, clearly deep in thought.

After dinner, Gerrin retired to his room. His living quarters were sectioned off from the rest of the basement and were in the farthest corner across from the stairs. He didn't have much: just a bed, dresser, a nightstand, and a mirror. Gerrin eased himself into bed and rested his head upon his pillow. For hours he tossed and turned. He needed to get some sleep, but he simply couldn't keep his mind from racing. Over and over Gerrin's mind circled the idea of leaving his home behind. Taking his family and moving them beyond Nox's reach wasn't a new idea for Gerrin, but up until now, it had always felt like an impossibility. Now it felt attainable.

His mind began to wander, recalling the many distant lands his parents would tell him and his sisters about when they returned from their travels. The more Gerrin thought, the more he started to imagine his family thriving in a new town. Safe. Sound. Happy. It was an intoxicating thought, one he was more than willing to indulge.

"Gerrin," Eissa whispered as she peered through the space between the stairs. "Are you still awake?"

"No," he whispered back. "I'm fast asleep."

Eissa giggled as she began walking down the stairs. Gerrin smiled and sat up on the edge of his bed. His sister might think he was a criminal, but he could still make her laugh.

"I take it you can't sleep either," he said.

Eissa shook her head and sat down alongside him. "I just . . . I'm so confused. Lysabel says you've been working for Nox, and you've been doing it for a while, but I don't understand." She turned to Gerrin, and his heart sank. Her eyes were watery and red. "Why would you do such a thing?"

Gerrin took a deep breath and told her the truth about his trips to Hastos and his deal with Nox. It was painful to say, and he felt more and more disgusted with himself the longer he spoke, but he kept on. It was the least he could do after lying to his sister for so long.

"So you did it for us," Eissa said, placing her hands on her lap.

"Well, yes. But that doesn't mean it's your fault or anything like that. It's something I chose to do to keep you all safe. I know it wasn't the brightest idea, but it's all I could think to do to protect you all. You and Gram and Lysabel mean the world to me. I would do anything for you guys."

"But I don't want you to be a bad person."

"What do you mean? It's not like I've hurt anyone. I've only smuggled drugs from time to time. It's not like I've done anything close to what Nox has over the years."

Eissa shook her head. "If you work for bad people doing bad things, that makes you a bad person. You might not be like Nox, but unless you stop working for him, you're a bad guy too."

Gerrin paused. For a second, he thought about telling Eissa the plan to leave Lasslail and how soon he wouldn't be working for Nox anymore, but his better judgment kicked in. Although he and Olenor hadn't discussed it in full, Gerrin knew that for his family to have the best chance to escape, Nox and his men had to think everything was business as usual.

It was undoubtedly the right call, but that didn't make looking into Eissa's despair-filled eyes any easier. She was a wreck. It was clear she was struggling to hold back her anguish, but at any moment, she could break down into countless bits of sorrow. Gerrin's throat was tight, and every impulse he had screamed for him to comfort his sister, to lift her weary spirit out of the sadness that gripped it like a vise.

"How did I know I'd find you down here?" Lysabel said, walking down the stairs.

Gerrin sighed, thankful for the distraction. "At this rate, we might as well invite Gram down and have a family meeting."

Eissa took a deep breath and wiped her eyes.

Lysabel placed a hand on her hip. "So, which one of them kicked your ass?"

"Lysabel!" Eissa exclaimed. "How many times has Gram scolded you for using such language?"

Lysabel rolled her eyes. "Gram is knocked out and couldn't hear me if I shouted it in her ear. Besides, Gerrin might be a bandit, but he's no snitch."

"I am not a bandit," Gerrin replied, his tone blunt and direct.

"Oh, I'm sorry. Let me make sure I use the proper terminology. Are you a thug? Or perhaps gangster is more to your liking?"

Gerrin scoffed. "Very funny."

"And yet no one is laughing. It's almost as if I wasn't joking."

"Look. I'm not proud of working for Nox, but like I was telling Eissa, I'm only doing it to keep you all safe."

Lysabel shook her head. "So you still plan on working for him even after they beat you senseless. I guess it's true what they say. You can't find good role models anymore."

Gerrin bit his tongue. Talking to Lysabel was always so much more challenging than Eissa. "I'm sorry, but—"

"Don't be sorry," Lysabel interrupted. "Be better. Do you think Mom and Dad would approve of what you're doing?"

Gerrin froze.

"Stop it," Eissa said, nearly choking on her words. "You shouldn't bring Mom and Dad into this."

Lysabel balled her fists. "Why not? Gerrin clearly didn't care about their legacy beforehand. Or maybe he just forgot that they fought against bandits. Maybe it slipped his mind that it was someone like Nox who took them away from us."

"Get out," Gerrin said, his voice low.

"I'm not leaving until—"

"I SAID GET OUT!"

The girls jumped at Gerrin's outburst. Eissa was the first to leave. She moved quickly, running up the stairs without looking back. For a moment Lysabel stayed, staring at her brother. It wasn't the first time Gerrin had yelled at her, and it certainly wouldn't be the last. This time was different, though. Lysabel's eyes began to water, and tears rolled down her cheeks. She wiped her eyes and left the basement, leaving Gerrin alone with his thoughts.

Gerrin took a breath as he tried to steady his nerves. He had thought about his parents, Seirrin and Nadya, nearly every day. Despite this, he had always tucked away the circumstances of their death deep in his mind. And with just a few words, Lysabel had unearthed everything he kept concealed. His heart beat faster, and he couldn't keep his hands from trembling. He turned to his nightstand. It was calling to him like a siren in the ocean. He tried to ignore it, but finally, he opened the drawer and pulled out a wooden picture frame.

It contained a picture of Gerrin's parents. They were young, in their mid-twenties. It was clear to see Gerrin and his sisters took after their father, apart from their eyes. Seirrin's were a dark blue.

On the other hand, Nadya was a short woman with jet black hair. She had eyes just like her kids', and her skin was a dark earthy brown. Seirrin wore elegant robes of white, gold, and red, while Nadya wore an equally graceful gown filled with frills and of the same colors. They were smiling ear to ear and held each other tightly.

Tears began to fall from Gerrin's eyes, landing on the picture frame.

"I'm sorry," he said, wiping away his tears. "I promise, I'm going to make things right."

CHAPTER 4
AN IMPOSSIBLE SITUATION (GERRIN POV)

Between his injuries and the emotional rollercoaster, Gerrin didn't get much sleep. Breakfast was beyond awkward. His sisters refused to look his way or even speak to him. Eissa kept to herself, focusing on her plate of pancakes, while Lysabel spoke only to Olenor. Unable to bear the tension, Gerrin took his food to his workshop. He wasn't scheduled to do anything for Nox, meaning he could focus on tending to the farm and working on the abandoned vehicle he had found in the desert.

After finishing his breakfast, he began trying to open the vehicle without damaging it. He worked slowly and with frequent grunts and gasps. His body ached and he probably would have been better taking the day off to rest. But if he could just get the car working again, it would serve much better than his dusty old truck for escaping Nox's grasp. He grew more frustrated with each attempt at merely opening the vehicle. Even still, he was determined to get it in working order and secure his family's safety.

"Gerrin!" Eissa exclaimed from behind him.

He turned around to find his sister at the barn's entrance. She held onto the door, panting and trembling. "What is it?" he asked as he approached his sister.

"Nox's men are here," she replied between heavy breaths.

Gerrin ground his teeth. "Stay here until they leave," he said, placing a hand on Eissa's shoulder.

Gerrin started to leave, only to stop when Eissa grabbed his arm. "Please," she said softly. "Promise me you won't leave with them."

He paused. Gerrin wanted desperately to turn to his sister and take her in his arms. He wanted to tell her that he was the brother she used to look up to, and he would never disappoint her again. But now wasn't the time.

"I'm sorry," he said, keeping his attention on the house, his voice cracking with emotion. "I can't make that promise. But I swear that one day you'll understand. Until that day...you'll just have to hate me."

Gerrin left the barn running through the melon field and back to the house. He moved as fast as he could manage, ignoring the aches he felt in his body. He could see Jabal along with three other men. Olenor and Lysabel were also present. Even at a distance and without making out what she was saying, he could tell Lysabel was being her usual rambunctious self, and it looked like Olenor was trying to defuse the situation but to no avail.

"What do you guys want?" Gerrin asked, approaching Jabal.

"Nox thinks it's time you get your feet wet doing some real work," Jabal began. "We've got word of a caravan dropping off supplies to Hastos. We're going to appropriate those resources for ourselves. It should be an easy enough job even for a pissant like you."

"Whatever," Gerrin said. "Just tell me when and where, and I'll be there."

"That's a good boy," Jabal said with a smile. "We're heading to The Respite now to go over the plans in greater detail."

"If you leave with them, I'll never forgive you," Lysabel said, her tone definitive and full of rage.

Gerrin turned to his sister. She stared directly at him with balled fists, and her nostrils flared.

"Lysabel," Olenor said, placing her hand on her granddaughter's shoulder. "We should go inside. This is no place—"

Lysabel pulled away. "No!" she shouted. "Gerrin has to choose. Either he's going to be a part of this family or theirs."

Gerrin turned around, afraid that if he looked at his sister for a moment longer, he would collapse into the sand. "Let's go," he said as he proceeded to walk away with the bandits.

He couldn't have made it more than a few steps before he heard Lysabel shouting behind him.

"You're a fucking coward, Gerrin! You and all the other bandits! You think you're real men beating down people who can't defend themselves! You're nothing but cockroaches who need to just roll over and die!"

As much as her words stung, Gerrin kept walking, ignoring his sister lashing out behind him.

"You know," Jabal began as he stopped and turned around. "I think this is a perfect opportunity for you to show us just where your loyalties lie."

Jabal then removed the revolvers from his hip holsters and held out one of them towards Gerrin, prompting him to take it.

Gerrin looked down at the gun and swallowed the lump in his throat. "What do you want me to do with that?" he asked, as if he didn't already know the answer.

Jabal aimed his other gun at Gerrin. "Shoot her, or I will put a bullet in each of them."

Gerrin couldn't see Jabal's eyes behind his sunglasses, but he didn't need to. Everything about the bandit evidenced that he meant business. The way he stood with intent, his attention set on Gerrin and Gerrin alone. The clarity in his tone that left no room for misinterpretation. The way he held his pistol aimed squarely at Gerrin's chest.

"You must be joking," he said, forcing a chuckle. "You can't expect—"

Jabal pulled the hammer back on his revolver, and the click it made sent shivers through Gerrin's body.

"I've never been a funny guy," Jabal said. "You have ten seconds to decide. You kill the brat, or I kill everyone. What's it gonna be?"

The air was tense, and nobody moved as Gerrin stared at the gun in Jabal's hand. It was quiet, say for the whistling of the arid breeze tossing sand around.

Gerrin ground his teeth. "Is this really necessary?" he asked. "I already said I would do the job."

"Ten . . . nine . . . eight . . ."

"Jabal," Gerrin said taking a step toward him.

Jabal pulled the trigger, and a gunshot echoed throughout the farm. Gerrin's heart nearly jumped out of his chest. He looked down, expecting to find a bullet wound, but found nothing. He spun around, praying his grandmother and sister were still standing. Olenor was shielding Lysabel with her body. They were trembling, but they otherwise seemed unharmed. Jabal's precision with a pistol was surgical. There was no way he had missed accidentally.

"Seven . . . six . . ."

Gerrin turned back to Jabal. His skin felt tight, and his shoulders were tense. His heart was pulsing so much so he could hear it thumping in his ears. He took the gun. It couldn't have been more than a pound, but it felt like a hundred.

"Five . . . four . . ."

Gerrin's mind was a tangled mess while he tried to figure a way out of the situation. He wondered if he'd be able to shoot Jabal before Jabal shot him. No. That was impossible. But maybe Gerrin could fire off a few shots as he went down. It was certain death, but he might be able to hold on just long enough to take

Jabal with him. No, that wasn't an option. Even if he managed to take Jabal down with him, there'd be no one left to protect his family. Nox and his men would be free to do whatever they wanted.

"Three..."

Gerrin ground his teeth once more, breathing deep through his nostrils.

"Two..."

"Forgive me," Gerrin said softly. He pulled the hammer back on the revolver, and with teary eyes, he looked at Jabal.

"One..."

"Excuse me," a woman said faintly staggering out of the melon fields.

She was a woman of average height with sandy brown skin and eyes like fresh limes. Her hair was a mess of licorice-colored curls sprouting in every direction. Despite her lean frame, she was quite muscular. Around her waist wrapped a pale gray skirt fashioned from a wolf's pelt, under which she wore a pair of black tights and dark gray boots. Her red long-sleeved crop top jacket was tied in a small knot, exposing a set of hardened abs.

"Nox won't be pleased," Jabal said. Hhe aimed his gun behind him, all the while keeping his eyes on Gerrin. "You know outsiders aren't allowed in Lasslail."

Jabal shot the woman in the dead center of her forehead despite not looking. As the bullet hit her skin, she began to glow with jagged blue lines. The dented bullet fell into the sand, but she was unharmed.

The woman balled her fist, and her forehead wrinkled with her scowl. "If there's one thing I can't stand," she said, her tone falling low and filling with irritation, "it's being shot at."

"Interesting." Jabal glanced back over his shoulder. "I didn't miss, and yet you're still standing."

Gerrin raised his gun, pointing it at Jabal's head. He squeezed the trigger, and the gun fired. Jabal moved out the way with a twist, dodging the bullet entirely. He aimed his weapon at Gerrin. In the blink of an eye, the woman dashed forward. Her body glowed with jagged red lines before throwing a kick. Her leg collided with Jabal's arm. He yelped and flew across the sand like a rocket. Jabal's men drew their weapons on the woman and opened fire. The red glow turned blue. Just like before, the bullets hit her skin but had no effect.

The woman glared at Jabal's men. When Gerrin looked at her, her gaze sent lightning was dancing across his skin. She walked towards them. Each slow step she took rattled the ground beneath her feet. Jabal's men broke into a panic. Tripping over themselves, they ran to collect the unconscious Jabal and retreated to the village.

Gerrin, Olenor, and Lysabel watched in shock while the bandits ran away, cowering in fear. The woman collapsed, falling backward into the sand. Gerrin sprang forward and rushed to her side. "Miss, are you okay? You're not hurt, are you?"

"Not at all," the woman said, flashing a smile as bright as an supernova. "But I am hungry. You wouldn't happen to have any meat, would you?"

Gerrin fell silent, unsure of how to respond.

"We certainly do," Olenor said. "I hope you like beef."

"Beef. Chicken. Bear. As long as it doesn't talk, I'll eat it."

Olenor began walking back towards the house. "Don't just sit there, Gerrin. Help the girl inside."

"R-right," Gerrin said. He helped the woman up and turned to Lysabel. "Eissa's hiding in my workshop. Could you go—"

Lysabel rushed over and threw her arms around Gerrin. She held him tightly and wept, her tears soaking into his shirt. "I'm so sorry," she sobbed. "I've been a horrible sister."

"You didn't do anything wrong." Gerrin returned her embrace. "I let you down. Remember?"

Lysabel shook her head. "I said terrible things to you. You could have died and—"

"And nothing you say could ever make me love you any less." Gently Gerrin pulled Lysabel back. "Now go get your sister. With all that gunfire, she's probably worried out of her mind."

Lysabel sniffled and wiped the tears from her eyes. "I love you too," she said before heading off to the barn.

"That's sweet," the woman said. "Reminds me of my brother."

"I owe you one," Gerrin said.

The woman shook her head. "Not really. It's not like I was trying to save you or anything like that."

"Excuse me?" Gerrin said, perplexed.

"I said I wasn't trying to save you."

"No, I heard you. I just . . . I guess I wasn't expecting that response."

"Oh. Okay then."

"So, if you didn't care to save us, why did you get involved then? Strike that. Where did you even come from? You're obviously not from Lasslail."

"Lasslail?" the woman said with a groan. "I was trying to get to Baradir."

"Miss, you do realize you're in the Hastos desert? Right?"

"I do now. I thought Baradir was to the east."

"It is. The Hastos Desert is to the west."

The woman tilted her head back in frustration. "Damn it."

Gerrin paused while he looked at her. She was an enigma, and the more he tried to wrap his head around the idea of her, the farther the concept seemed to drift away. Mere moments ago, she had seemed like a champion reaching into the soul-crushing darkness to lift Gerrin's family into the light. But now, she resisted his attempts to comprehend her, like the eldest tree in an ever-expanding forest.

"So, how far is Baradir from here?" the woman asked.

Gerrin snapped back into the conversation. "It's, uh, pretty far."

"Oh well," the woman said with a shrug and a smile. "At least I got to see the desert. You always gotta look at the silver lining."

They both went inside, taking a seat at the dining room table. The enchanting smells emanating from the kitchen made the entire house smell like a bistro.

Gerrin recalled his manners. "I'm sorry. My name's Gerrin Ruu. The woman in the kitchen is my grandmother, Olenor, and the young girl you saw outside is my sister Lysabel. I have another sister named Eissa who should be coming in any minute."

"My name is Ksara Sepheron," the woman replied, holding out her hand. "It's a pleasure to meetcha."

Gerrin shook Ksara's hand, wincing as her grip nearly crushed his hand. "I know you said not to thank you, but in all honesty, if you hadn't come around, I'd be a dead man."

Ksara sighed and let go of Gerrin's hand. "If you're not going to let it go, then I guess you're welcome. But really, I'm no hero. I just don't like being shot at. Really grinds my gears. You know?"

"Yeah . . . So, I get you're incredibly lost, but what are you doing here on our farm?"

"Well, I was traveling through the desert, and my ship broke down in the middle of a sandstorm. I hunkered down and tried to wait things out, but I kind of ran out of supplies, and the heat didn't exactly help either."

"Wait a minute. You were in that vehicle I found?"

Ksara smiled and nodded. "Yup. That's my ship. I call her the *Eclipse*."

Gerrin chuckled. "You keep saying ship. Don't you think that's a little ambitious?"

"What do you mean?" Ksara asked, a look of bewilderment clear across her face.

"I mean, your *ship* is a little small."

"And?"

"And one might consider her too small to be classified as a ship."

Ksara looked sternly into Gerrin's eyes. "Well, when you're a bandit, people don't tend to disagree with you."

CHAPTER 5
A MUTUALLY BENEFICIAL ARRANGEMENT
(GERRIN POV)

Gerrin's heart skipped a beat, and his stomach dropped like a lead ball. He stared at Ksara, struggling processing what he had heard. Was she really a bandit? Lasslail was already in ruins. Just what would another bandit bring to the village's misfortune?

Ksara smiled and patted Gerrin on the shoulder. He nearly fell out of his seat. It wasn't clear whether she had overestimated Gerrin's strength or underestimated her own. Either way, his shoulder hurt like hell.

"You know I'm just kidding. Right?" Ksara said with a grin.

Gerrin forced a chuckle, and his stomach began to unknot itself. "Yeah . . . I knew that."

"I know the *Eclipse* isn't a ship, but she's all I have for now." She smirked. "One day, I'll have the grandest ship of all the bandits who ever lived."

As quickly as relief came, it was gone again. "So, you are a bandit then?" Gerrin asked.

"Of course. Isn't it obvious?"

"Get out."

"No, really. I've been a bandit since I was ten. I served under the great Captain Elpys before he let me go to form my own crew."

"No," Gerrin said, his fists balled as he stood up, "I meant—"

Olenor placed a hand on his shoulder, approaching the table with a steaming plate of steak and potatoes. "Gerrin," she said as she put the plate down in front of Ksara, "Could I get your help over in the kitchen for a moment? The icemaker is doing that thing again."

Gerrin turned to his grandmother only to find that monstrous glare that meant intolerable suffering would be coming his way if he didn't comply. Gerrin walked over to the freezer with Olenor and opened it. It was working just fine.

"Don't go chasing that girl off," Olenor whispered. She then handed Gerrin an empty glass.

"She's a bandit," Gerrin whispered back. "We're still dealing with the whole Nox situation, which I'll remind you isn't exactly going well. The last thing we need is another one. Honestly, we should just send her off to the village, get the girls in the truck, and take off. If we're lucky, they'll all be too distracted to notice us booking it out of town."

"Ksara is not like the other bandits."

Gerrin filled the glass with ice and then water. "You don't know that. She literally just showed up on the farm. She could be just like Nox. Maybe even worse."

"Do you really believe that?"

Gerrin looked over at Ksara. She was laser-focused on her plate. Her eyes glistened as she devoured her meal, and it was clear she was savoring every bite.

"No," Gerrin said with a sigh.

"Exactly. I have a feeling this woman might be the perfect solution to our village's problems."

Gerrin pursed his lips before returning to the table. He sat the glass of water next to Ksara's plate and took his seat. "I'm sure you noticed we have a bandit problem in Lasslail," Gerrin said.

"You mean the guys who shot at me," Ksara said between bites. "I wouldn't call them bandits."

"Well, they call themselves The Flame Bandits and first came to Lasslail about six years ago. They've been a nuisance ever since. In all honesty, my family planned to flee this village using your ship. You see—"

Ksara whipped towards Gerrin, glaring at him like an angry hyena. "You were going to steal my ship?"

Gerrin swallowed the lump in his throat. "Not, not exactly," he replied with a stutter. "I thought it was abandoned. It was in the middle of the desert, after all."

"It wasn't abandoned," Ksara said, driving her fork through a chunk of meat. "I was inside."

"And how was I supposed to know that? Your ship is impenetrable from the outside. I spent all morning trying to break into it so I could see what repairs I'd need to make, but I got absolutely nowhere."

Ksara grabbed her water and took a sip, "I guess that's true. It'd take a hell of a lot to get through the security system. Wait. You said something about repairs."

"Yeah. I'm something of a mechanic."

"Gerrin's being modest," Olenor said. "He's been a tinkerer ever since he was little. Gets it from his father. I can't tell you how many times I've caught him taking something apart just to put it back together."

Gerrin blushed and he rubbed the back of his neck. "I'm self-taught...but I do keep my truck and all the equipment on the farm running. Your ship is like nothing I've ever seen, but I'm sure with enough time, I could figure it out."

Ksara's eyes lit up, and she grabbed Gerrin's hands. "You can fix my ship then! This isn't the first time the *Eclipse* has broken down on me. It is the worst, though. It's been weeks since I had anything to eat or drink."

"Sure," Gerrin said, startled by Ksara's outburst. "But we're going to need something from you first."

Ksara pouted. "I'm afraid I don't have any money. Would you be willing to fix it, and I'll pay you back later?"

Gerrin shook his head. "We don't want any money, but I do have something else in mind. If you would get rid of the Flame Bandits for us, I'll gladly do whatever I can to fix your ship."

"Okay."

"Okay?"

"Yeah. That sounds like a good deal to me. Do you not agree? I mean, you did come up with it."

"No, I do. I just . . . I didn't expect you to agree so easily."

"Why not? You have the harder job. All I have to do is knock around a few guys pretending to be bandits."

"I suppose that's one way to look at it."

"Actually, I would like to alter the deal a little."

Gerrin sighed, irritated with himself for being so caught off guard. "What else would you like?"

"In addition to fixing my ship," Ksara said, "I'd like more meat. And lots of it."

Olenor laughed. "If you get rid of the bandits. I'll make sure you get all the meat you can stomach."

Ksara flashed a huge smile and stood up. "All righty then. Where can I find these *bandits*?"

"Wait a minute," Gerrin said as he stood up as well. "You should know about their leader, Nox. You see, he has this spark—"

Ksara stretched her shoulders. "I don't really care what his spark is. I just need you to tell me where I can find him."

Once again, Gerrin found himself looking at Ksara in complete bewilderment, but he was distracted by motion in the window behind her. A group of people were heading towards the house. He walked outside to find the village elder leading several other villagers.

"Gerrin," the village elder said. "We've heard you've brought an outsider into Lasslail."

Gerrin opened his mouth to speak, but Ksara beat him to it. "That would be me. The name's Ksara Sepheron."

The crowd erupted into whispers.

"Then is it also true that this outsider, er, Ksara . . . you defeated Nox's second in command?"

"That's right. He shot me, so I broke his arm."

The whispers grew to chatters.

"Yeah," Gerrin said with a chuckle. "Ksara really doesn't like being shot."

The village elder kneeled. He looked down and placed his palms on the sand. "Please, Miss Ksara," he began. "Please rid our town of Nox and his men."

"That's not necessary, elder," Gerrin said. "Ksara already agreed to get rid of the bandits."

Ksara slapped Gerrin in his arm, and he winced in pain. "Shh. I could make another deal for more meat."

"Could you please stop hitting me with your freakishly strong hands?" Gerrin rubbed his arm.

Ksara giggled. "Sorry about that."

"Thank you," the village elder said.

The rest of the crowd joined in, thanking Ksara for saving Lasslail and celebrating that they would soon be rid of their troubles.

"Calm down, everyone," Ksara said. "Don't get the wrong idea here. I'm just fulfilling my end of a bargain."

The crowd turned quiet, and confusion took over.

"She's right," Gerrin said. "Ksara is a bandit herself. She only agreed to help because I promised to fix her ship if she drove the Flame Bandits out of Lasslail."

The crowd all looked at Ksara, waiting in bated breath for a response.

"It's true. I'm a bandit through and through and have no qualms doing as I please, taking whatever my heart desires."

Fear washed over the crowd. You could almost see the shred of hope they carried fade away.

"But like Gerrin said," she continued, "we've struck a deal, and I'll be taking care of these so-called bandits. You all can rest easy, though. I have no interest in Lasslail. Once my ship is all fixed, I'll be heading straight to Baradir and then Mithrandir."

The crowd perked up, reinvigorated by Ksara's words.

Olenor dashed out of the house, clearly in a panic. "Are Lysabel and Eissa with you?"

Gerrin turned to his grandmother. "No," he replied. "I sent Lysabel to grab Eissa out of the barn."

Realization hit him like an anvil crushing an acorn. It had been ages since Lysabel had gone off to the barn, and she should certainly have returned by now.

CHAPTER 6

KSARA VS. THE FLAME BANDITS (KSARA POV)

Ksara opened her mouth to speak, but Gerrin bolted toward the barn. "Wait a minute," she called out to him.

He didn't respond, so she ran after him. She approached the barn door and heard loud clanks and rustling. Ksara entered to find Gerrin frantically searching, knocking over machinery and equipment as he looked for any sign of his sisters, but not a trace of them remained.

Gerrin paused in the middle of the barn. He was silent, and it looked as if he were lost in a raging sea of thoughts and emotion. Even still, he didn't need to say a word for Ksara to know precisely what was going through his mind. His legs buckled, and Ksara rushed over to keep him from collapsing. He trembled, fists balled so tightly it was a miracle he didn't puncture the palms of his hands.

Gerrin looked at Ksara with teary eyes, and she flashed a smile. "Tell me where I can find Nox," she said.

For a moment, he just stood there, but with each second that passed, Ksara could feel Gerrin's shoulders loosen. He unclenched his fists and began walking towards the door.

"I'm sure he's at the village saloon." He reached into his pocket and pulled out his keys. "Let's go."

Ksara followed Gerrin over to his truck. "Are you sure you want to come along?" she asked, sitting down in the passenger seat. "You don't exactly look like you're in peak fighting condition."

"There's no way I'm staying here while my sisters are in danger."

Ksara grinned and leaned back in her seat, placing her feet on the dash. "Watch yourself out there. Remember, you promised to fix my ship."

Gerrin nodded and the two sped off, heading to The Respite. Nox and his men were outside huddled into a crowd. Apart from himself and Aegar, the bandits were all armed with guns.

"Nox!" Gerrin shouted, slamming his truck door behind him. "Where are they?"

Ksara walked up next to Gerrin, scanning the crowd. She shook her head and smiled as she cracked her knuckles. "This is going to be too easy."

The gang of people parted, revealing Nox and Aegar standing next to Lysabel and Eissa. The girls were gagged and bound to the posts holding up the saloon awning.

"Let them go!" Gerrin tightened his fists.

"I was wondering when you'd turn up." Nox turned towards Eissa and ran a finger across her face. She winced, screaming through the rag in her mouth. Lysabel struggled against her binding, trying with all her might to break free.

Gerrin took off running towards Nox, but he didn't get very far. Ksara grabbed his arm and tossed him back behind the truck, saving him from a hailstorm of bullets. Gunfire rang throughout the village as Nox's men fired shot after shot at Ksara, but each bullet that hit her did nothing but piss her off.

"What part of 'I don't like being shot at' don't you all understand?" she snarled.

The gunfire stopped while the men began to reload. She leaped high into the air above the crowd. She approached the ground and swung her foot, planting it into the sand.

The entire village shook as if a meteor had struck the ground. A crater formed at the heart of the impact, swallowing the bulk of Nox's men. Sand rose into the air and fell back to the ground like powdered snow. Brushing dirt off her shoulder, Ksara walked out of the sandy clouds. She glared at the remainder of Nox's men like a wolf cornering her prey.

"B-boss," one of the men stammered, backing up towards his leader. "Maybe—maybe we should retreat."

Nox reached out and placed a hand on the man's back. The lackey burst into flames. Dropping his weapon, he hit the ground and began to roll from side to side, all the while crying out in agony. The desert sand should have been the perfect means to snuff out the flames. And yet, he continued to burn until his body was nothing but charred flesh, and a deafening silence overtook the air.

Ksara looked down at the burnt body. A scowl overtook her face and she tightened her fists. "I knew none of you were really bandits," she said, contempt evident in her tone. "But killing your own men..."

Nox smirked. "If I'm not a bandit, then what would you call me?"

"I don't know what you call a leader sick enough murder someone who has pledged their lives to them. 'Rat' comes to mind, but that just feels offensive to rodents."

"A leader has no use for the weak. This pathetic excuse for a henchman signed his death warrant the second he thought of abandoning this fight."

"You're wrong. A true leader takes care of their people above all else. They would gladly suffer a thousand deaths to spare the life of one of their own."

Nox burst into laughter. "Foolish girl." He wiped a tear from his eye. "What kind of king sacrifices himself for his pawns?"

"You're the fool. A king would never refer to his people like that."

"Step aside," Nox said to his men. "Let Aegar handle this."

Nox's men stepped back and Aegar moved forward. "You got it, boss. I'll make this quick."

"Move out of my way," Ksara said walking towards Aegar.

He didn't respond and instead threw a punch at her. She returned the blow, and their knuckles collided with a bone-shattering crunch. Aegar cried out, his fist crumbled. He stumbled backward holding his mangled hand and blubbered like an injured child.

"I said *move out of my way!*" Ksara grabbed Aegar by his tunic, lifted the behemoth into the air, and tossed him into the crater behind her.

Nox's men fled, dropping their weapons and running away from the saloon. Ksara began walking towards Nox. He ducked behind Lysabel and Eissa and held his palms mere inches from their throats.

"Stay back," Nox said as his fists ignited in flames. His voice was full of desperation, and he was sweating profusely.

Ksara stopped. She smiled and folded her arms. "It took you long enough."

Bewilderment washed over Nox's features, but it didn't last long. A gunshot rang out, and his face vanished into a cloud of blood and brains while a bullet pierced through the back of his head. Gerrin stood over Nox's corpse slumped over onto Lysabel and Eissa, Jabal's smoking revolver firmly grasped in his hand.

The twins were hysterical and splattered with gore. Gerrin pulled the lifeless bandit off them and got to work untying the ropes. Ksara rushed over to the trio of siblings and gave Gerrin a hand. Once freed, Lysabel and Eissa took their brother into their arms. None of them spoke, but their tears fell in a downpour.

The saloon doors swung open, and out limped Jabal. Gerrin stepped forward, moving his sisters behind him, and aimed his gun toward Jabal. However, Ksara reached over and placed her hand on the gun's barrel.

"What are you doing?" Gerrin said.

"Trust me," she replied.

With a reluctant scowl, Gerrin released his hold on the gun.

Ksara walked over to Jabal. "I take it this belongs to you?" She held out the gun's handle.

"Who would have thought it'd be one of my guns that did him in." Jabal took his weapon and holstered it, then looked over at Gerrin and his sisters. "You don't have to worry. I'm a man of my word. As of this moment, the Flame Bandits are no more and will be leaving Lasslail. Although, to be honest, it looks like there isn't much left for me to disband."

Jabal walked over to Nox and got down on one knee. For a moment, he struggled to place Nox onto his shoulder on account of his injured arm. Ksara lifted Nox's body onto Jabal's back.

"Thank you," Jabal said as he stood up.

Ksara turned away. "Don't thank me. This man is a disgrace to bandits, and if it were up to me, I'd dump his body in the desert to rot." She sighed, placing a hand on her hip. "But he's your family. That should be your decision to make."

With Nox's body on his back, Jabal left the saloon heading out of Lasslail. He entered the desert, and before long it became impossible to spot him in the distance.

CHAPTER 7
CELEBRATION (KSARA POV)

News of the Flame Bandits' defeat spread through Lasslail like a wildfire. That night, the village overflowed with jubilee. The village elder banded the residents together, and the villagers put on a massive feast. Several tents in the middle of the village, each of them filled with tables and chairs, encircled a massive bonfire. Not a single glass remained empty for very long.

For hours, the festivities raged on and showed no signs of slowing down. Gerrin, Lysabel, Eissa and Ksara sat at the far end of a table. Gerrin and his sisters had already eaten their fill. Ksara, however, was working on her third plate of food and a fourth pitcher of ale.

"It's like this." She placed a cleaned drumstick onto her plate. "My spark allows my body to absorb kinetic energy. I can then take that energy, multiply it, and do all sorts of things with it."

"You mean like, punch somebody really really hard," Eissa said.

"Yeah," Ksara replied. She then held her middle finger back with her thumb. "Or I can do something like this."

Ksara aimed her finger at Eissa. Jagged red lines appeared on her body.

"It all happens first in my mind, visualizing what I need my body to do. It helps to think of my stored energy like a river my brain directs wherever I need it to go."

Ksara released her finger. A gust of wind flew forth, rustling Eissa's hair.

"That's so cool!" Lysabel exclaimed.

"Yeah," Eissa agreed. "You're practically invincible."

"I wouldn't say that," Ksara replied. "There are limits how much energy I can store and output, but in any case, I'm just a bitch and a half to put down."

"I hope I develop a spark like yours," Lysabel said. "If I were as strong as you, I could protect Lasslail all on my own."

Eissa chuckled. "That's unlikely."

Lysabel scoffed. "It's not that unlikely."

"We're already fifteen and haven't developed one. Plus, Gerrin's nineteen and he doesn't have a spark either."

"So?"

"So I think it's safe to say we will be sparkless too."

"They do say that if you don't develop a spark by eighteen, you're not going to," Ksara said. She took her pitcher of ale. In one breath, she swallowed the contents of the pitcher whole and signaled for another. "But just because you don't have a spark doesn't mean you can't grow to be strong. Before I left to start my own crew, I served under the strongest bandit captain in all the realms who just so happened to be sparkless."

"It's still so hard to believe that you're a bandit," Eissa said.

"Yeah," Lysabel said. "Are you sure you're a bandit? You're really not like any I've ever met before."

Ksara laughed with a loud snort as she took a fresh pitcher from a waitress. "I'm as sure as my name is Ksara." Once again, she drank the entire pitcher in a single breath and gasped for air once she was done.

"So, how did you become a bandit?" Lysabel asked.

Ksara opened her mouth to speak, but Gerrin cut her off. "Girls, it's getting late. We should head home and get some sleep."

"Come on, Gerrin," Eissa replied with a whine.

"Yeah," Lysabel said. "Don't you think tonight counts as a special night, and curfews shouldn't apply?"

"Sure," Gerrin said. "But I'm not Gram, and if you two aren't back at the farm at a somewhat reasonable time, she's going to murder all three of us."

The girls groaned while they stood up and pushed in their chairs.

"Don't worry," Gerrin continued, standing up. "Ksara will be staying with us until her ship's fixed. I'm sure by the time she leaves, you'll know everything there is to know about her."

"Your brother's right," Ksara said with a hiccup and a slur in her words.

She tried to stand, but her balance was off, forcing her to hold onto the table. She felt warm and tingly, and it looked as if everything around her was swaying back and forth. Her mind was a blur, and she found it an impossible task to focus on one thought for very long.

"Okay," Gerrin said. He took Ksara by the hand. "Somebody's a little drunk."

Ksara shook her head. "No!" she exclaimed. "I'm not drunk! I'm . . . I'm just not very sober right now."

Gerrin chuckled. "That, by definition, is what drunk is."

"No. No. See, my Captain Elpys used to say that, that if you can still drink . . . if, if you can still drink, then you're not drunk yet."

Ksara looked around and waved down the waitress. "I'll prove it," she said. "Waitress . . . get me another pitcher."

Gerrin turned to the waitress and shook his head. "Yeah, that's gonna be a no." He reached into his jeans and pulled out his keys. "Could you pull the truck around?" he asked, tossing his keys to Lysabel.

"I'm all right," Ksara said. She stepped away from the table, only to stumble onto her knees. She turned to Gerrin and frowned. "Okay. I might be a little drunk."

Gerrin reached down and helped Ksara back to her feet. "Well, I would hope so after drinking five pitchers."

Ksara began to giggle. "That's it! I figured it out, Gerrin."

"And what did you figure out exactly?"

"It all makes sense now. I should have stopped at four pitchers."

Gerrin smiled. "Is that right?"

"Yes. Remember that for next time. Okay?"

"Next time?"

"Yes, Gerrin. The next time we go drinking together. Remember . . . four is the magic number. Not five. Four. Four-ah. Have you ever noticed, how four...it—it's more than three."

"Yeah. Try to not freak out. But five...it's more than four."

"You're right. Shit. It's more than three too."

Lysabel pulled up with the truck. Ksara tried to walk with support from Gerrin, but her legs simply wouldn't comply.

"All right." Gerrin braced himself. His knees wobbled and he stumbled, but he managed to lift Ksara and cradled her in his arms. "Let's get you to bed."

"You don't have to do this," she said. "I could . . . I could crawl over to the truck. Yeah. It's not that far."

"I'm not gonna let the woman who saved my village crawl around in the dirt. Carrying you is the least I can do."

"But you're hurt."

Gerrin blew out a puff of air. "I look a lot worse than I am. A good night's sleep and I'll be as good as new."

Gerrin carried Ksara over to the vehicle and laid her down in the truck bed. After climbing in, he tapped Lysabel's shoulder, and they pulled away.

Ksara looked up as the truck sped through Lasslail. The night sky was a canvas painted with vibrant shades of purple and red. There were no clouds, making the stars more visible. A sense of deja vu washed over her. In her travels aboard the *Horizon*, Ksara had spent many nights gazing upon skies just like this. Perhaps it was the abundance of alcohol flowing through her veins. Or maybe it was the overwhelming comfort she felt welling up inside her. Whatever the case, she looked over, expecting to find her captain, but of course, it was only Gerrin.

"Is everything all right?" he asked. "If you have to hurl, let me know, and I'll have Lysabel pull the truck over."

Ksara sat up. "Come with me to Mithrandir."

"What?" Gerrin said, clearly shocked.

"I want you to join my crew and help me find the Heart of Mithrandir."

Gerrin chuckled. "You're a lot drunker than I thought you were."

"I told you I'm only a little drunk. And what does that have to do with anything anyway?"

"You don't know what you're talking about. Hell, I doubt you'll even remember this conversation in the morning."

Ksara pouted. "I know exactly what I'm talking about, and I'm not going to forget."

"Sure thing," Gerrin replied with a smirk.

"Every good ship needs a mechanic to keep it running smoothly. You could be that for the *Eclipse*."

"Despite working with them for several years, I'm not what you would call bandit material. And besides, my place is here in Lasslail, taking care of my family. You're better off finding someone else more suitable for the job."

"I don't want anyone else. I want you."

"I admit, I owe you a lot. A lot more than just a fixed ship. But still. I can't just leave my family behind. They need me to take care of them."

"I have a feeling they'd be okay with it," Ksara replied with a smile. "But I get it. Take some time to think it over. Like you said, I'll be staying with you for a while."

For a moment, they allowed silence to take hold between them, until Gerrin spoke once more. "Why me?" he asked.

"Why?"

Gerrin nodded. "I want to know why you want me in your crew. It's obvious I'm not like you, and if your goal is really to find the Heart of Mithrandir, a mechanic better equipped to enter the inner realm would be much more useful to you than some tinkerer from a small village in the middle of nowhere. So why are you so insistent on me joining your crew?"

Ksara laughed. "We're more alike than you realize . . . but the reason I want you in my crew is this moment right here and what I feel in my heart."

Gerrin flushed red and turned away. "Wha-what do you mean?"

"I've been traveling on my own for years now, and I've looked up at the night sky many times. You'd think this time would be just like the others, but it's not. I feel the same way I used to feel traveling with my captain aboard the *Horizon*." Ksara began to tear up; however, she wiped her eyes before they had a chance to fall. "If you were to join my crew, I could feel like this all the time."

"You still call him your captain. Even though you're building your own crew?"

Ksara nodded. "After everything he's done for me, Elpys will always be my captain."

"Is he—"

"Yes," Ksara replied. Her tone was low, laced with a wounded sharpness.

"I'm sorry. I shouldn't have pried."

"It's okay. I know I'll see Elpys again. They say you can find whatever your heart desires at the Heart of Mithrandir. That means he's there, and all I have to do is find him."

CHAPTER 8
OPTIONS (GERRIN POV)

Gerrin's truck pulled up to the farm. He could still hear the town partying the night away, even at a distance.

"All right," Gerrin said turning to Ksara. "Let's get you inside."

Ksara didn't respond. Gerrin prodded her shoulder with a gentle nudge only to find that she was fast asleep. He carried her inside to his room and placed her in his bed. He pulled the blanket over her and she took a deep breath, cozying up with his pillow. Gerrin couldn't help but smile as he turned and headed back upstairs.

Gerrin lay down on the living room sofa and placed his feet on the armrest. It had undoubtedly been a long, eventful day and he should have been too tired to keep his eyes open. And yet, sleep was the last thing on his mind. *Come with me to Mithrandir.* The words kept echoing through his mind like a broken record. Could he really just pack everything up and leave his family behind?

He turned over, faced the cushions, and closed his eyes. It couldn't have been more than five minutes before he turned again and turned once more ten minutes after that. Even though exhaustion began to set in, he found it an impossible task to fall asleep and stay that way for very long. By the time morning came, he had amassed maybe two hours of sleep. He could hear Olenor hard at work preparing breakfast for everyone, so he dragged himself off the couch and walked into the kitchen.

"Good morning." Olenor stirred a pan full of scrambled eggs.

Gerrin grabbed a can of coffee grounds out of a cabinet. "Good morning" he said with a yawn.

"Sounds like you had a long night."

Gerrin nodded and opened the can, allowing the pungent aroma of coffee to flood his nostrils. "I'll be all right," he said while he began to measure the grounds.

"Are you sure? Yesterday wasn't exactly an easy day."

"I'm sure."

Olenor plated the eggs before crossing the room to Gerrin. She placed a hand on his cheek and smiled. "You remind me so much of your father."

"Th-thank you," Gerrin replied with a flush rising in his cheeks.

"Your father was the type of man to shoulder everyone's problems." She walked over to a cabinet and pulled out a mug. "He would take everything the world threw at him, bury it deep inside, and ask what else he could do for those around him." Olenor let out a heavy sigh and handed Gerrin the mug. "It was his blessing . . . and his curse."

Gerrin fell silent, unsure of how to respond.

"I heard you fired the bullet that killed Nox," Olenor continued. "That isn't something to take lightly and certainly not something you should bottle up."

The moment he pulled the trigger flashed through Gerrin's mind in a series of sensory impressions. Jabal's gun and how heavy it felt in his hand. His sisters and the helpless, terrified look plastered on their faces. The blood spraying outward. "Nox was a menace to Lasslail. I did what I had to do to protect our family. My only regret is not doing it sooner."

"I'm not saying he didn't deserve it, or that what you did was wrong, but you're just a man, Gerrin. An amazing one, but still just a man. You've had an immeasurable pressure upon your shoulders for a long time. Even though you've lost that weight, you had to remove it yourself through violence. If you want to talk about it, I am here to listen."

"Thank you," Gerrin said, pouring himself a cup of coffee. "But I promise you I'm fine. I was actually up all night thinking about Ksara."

"Oh," Olenor said with a raised inflection. "I didn't realize you felt that way about her. You two only just met. Although, I suppose she is cute in her own sort of way."

Gerrin laughed. "That's not it. Ksara asked me to join her crew."

Olenor opened up the fridge and pulled out a plate of sausage links. "Did she now?"

"She's on a mission to find the Heart of Mithrandir and wants me to come with her as her ship mechanic."

"So you were up all night debating whether or not you should take her up on the offer?"

"Yeah."

"And given the tired expression and desperation for caffeine, I take it you haven't come to a conclusion yet?"

Gerrin rubbed the back of his neck. "Well . . . yes and no."

"How does that work?" The cold sausage hit the pan with a sizzle. "Either you decide to go, or you decide to stay."

"Well, I wouldn't mind traveling with Ksara, taking care of her ship, and whatnot. I mean, I still remember all the stories my mom and dad used to tell when they came back from their travels, and I used to dream about seeing the realms for myself. Since the Flame Bandits came to Lasslail, I've just felt so stuck. But now that they're gone, I finally have a chance to move forward."

"So, it sounds like you'll be leaving Lasslail then."

Gerrin set down his cup of coffee. "I want to, but what will happen to you and the girls if I leave? What if another gang of bandits comes to the village? What if they're even worse than Nox? You'd all be defenseless."

Olenor sighed. "Did I ever mention you remind me of your father?"

"I'm being serious," Gerrin said with a roll of his eyes. "Anything could happen to you guys while I'm gone, and I don't know if I could live with myself if something were to happen and I wasn't here to do something about it."

"I know you're being serious, and so am I. You can't live your life worrying about the what-ifs of the world. If I were you, I'd take her up on the offer."

Gerrin picked up his coffee, chuckling before taking a sip. "It sounds like you don't want me around anymore. Am I that insufferable?"

Olenor smiled. "I always imagined you would leave this small village in the middle of nowhere and follow in your parents' footsteps. What hurt most about bandits taking control of Lasslail was that they took you off your path and forced you to be someone you were never meant to be. But perhaps that was always what the world intended. I guess what I'm trying to say is, maybe joining Ksara's crew is what you're meant to do."

Gerrin paused, allowing Olenor's words to sink in.

"As your grandmother," she continued. "I support whatever decision you make. Even if it's the wrong one."

"Thank you," Gerrin said with a smile. "I'm gonna head off to the barn and get to work fixing Ksara's ship. Could you put a plate aside for me?"

"I'll try, but if you haven't noticed, that girl can eat. I don't know where she puts it all."

Gerrin left the kitchen heading to the basement. What he found in his room was an utter wreck. Ksara was sprawled out across his bed. His blanket only covered half of her body, and she was snoring like a rumbling chainsaw. Gerrin walked over and picked up his picture that had fallen off his nightstand. Thankfully, it was still intact. He smiled and returned the picture to its place.

"All right, princess." Gerrin gave Ksara a gentle shake. "Time to get up."

"Hmm," Ksara said as she slowly stirred awake.

"My grandma's cooking breakfast, and I need the keys to your ship."

"Does this breakfast include any meat?"

Gerrin laughed. "Yes. Now about those keys?"

Ksara sat up and let out a ferocious yawn. "My ship doesn't have keys."

"Then what does she have?" he asked with a raised brow.

"She doesn't have anything." Ksara then raised her right hand and grinned. "The *Eclipse* works when I touch her."

Gerrin let out a hefty sigh. "Okay then, I'll need you to come with me to the barn."

Slowly Ksara pulled herself out of bed and walked with Gerrin over to the barn. She approached the *Eclipse* and placed her palm onto the vehicle. The windows lost their tint, revealing the cockpit. There was a mass of screens, buttons, knobs, and sliders. A door handle popped out from the ship's side and Ksara opened the driver's side door. She then gestured Gerrin to take a seat.

"Your ship is unlike anything I've ever seen," Gerrin said, sitting down. He ran his fingers across the dashboard and a spark danced across the back of his neck. A smile stretched wide across his face while his gaze bounced around each shiny button begging to be pressed.

"You *can* fix her, though," Ksara said.

Gerrin cleared his throat. "I, uh, I should be able to. What's wrong with her?"

"Well, sometimes the *Eclipse* fails to start, and if I do manage to get her going, she'll will randomly power down."

"Sounds like an issue with the fuel system." Gerrin scanned over all the panels until he found a small screen about the size of his hand. "I'm guessing this is how you start her."

"Wait a minute."

It was too late. Gerrin had already placed his palm on the screen. All the panels flashed red, and a loud siren blared from the ship. Ksara reached over and put her hand on the screen. As soon as she touched it, the siren stopped, the panels turned green, and a steering wheel shot out from the dashboard in front of Gerrin. She drew a series of symbols on the screen with her fingertip, and the screen began to glow blue.

"All right," Ksara said. "Now you can place your hand on her."

Gerrin placed his palm on the screen. It began to scan his hand and, when finished, returned to its green hue.

"You now have full access to the *Eclipse*," Ksara continued. "Just place your hand on the screen to turn her on and hold it there to start the engine."

"This is incredible!" Gerrin exclaimed. "Where did you get a ship like this?"

"She used to belong to my captain." Ksara ran her hand across the *Eclipse* and smiled. "She was his dinghy. Well, she was one of them. My brother, Draec, owns his other one."

"Is he a bandit as well?"

"Of course."

"If you don't mind me asking, why aren't the two of you together? If you're both bandits, wouldn't you want to travel together?"

Ksara let out a hearty laugh. "Elpys used to say there are two types of people in the universe: those who are meant to lead and those who are meant to follow. Draec and I are both meant to lead. It's the reason why Elpys left us behind to form our own crews."

"I see. So is he looking for the Heart of Mithrandir, too?"

"Probably. To be honest, I haven't seen Draec in years. If he is searching for the Heart, I'm sure he's already made it to Mithrandir by now. He was always a better navigator than me." Ksara cracked her knuckles and smirked. "I could always kick his ass in a fight, though."

Gerrin couldn't help but laugh. "I should be good to get working. You can hang out here if you want, but I imagine Gram will be finished cooking soon."

Ksara licked her lips and rubbed her stomach. "You don't have to tell me twice." She started to leave the barn but turned back to face Gerrin. "By the way . . . I haven't forgotten about last night. I'm expecting an answer by the time you finish fixing the *Eclipse*."

Without waiting for a response, Ksara left the barn, and Gerrin got to work repairing the *Eclipse*. He pulled a red latch on the left side of the dashboard, causing a large panel to open on the *Eclipse's* hood. He got out of the vehicle and walked over to the open panel. There he found the ship's engine along with a massive battery and several other components. It was clear solar energy powered the vehicle, which put a smile on Gerrin's face. He didn't know exactly how to fix her just yet, but over his years on the farm, he had worked on solar-powered generators and was confident he would get her working again.

CHAPTER 9
ADVENTURE AWAITS (GERRIN POV)

After three long days, Gerrin had the *Eclipse* up and running again. He also had several conversations with his family. Each one inevitably led to the conclusion that he should leave Lasslail. Olenor, Eissa, and Lysabel agreed that if he were to become a member of Ksara's bandit crew, they would move to the safety of Hastos. The village elder even agreed to gather a party and help the family relocate.

Gerrin sat in his bed. Olenor was preparing a farewell dinner to send Ksara off on her way, and the girls were no doubt pestering the bandit leader with as many questions as they could fit in before they had to say goodbye. Gerrin took a deep breath and exhaled even deeper. He gazed at the picture of Seirrin and Nadya in his hands.

He could picture the day they left the farm for the last time so clearly. Lysabel was teasing Eissa for being so upset as if they hadn't taken trips to the inner realm countless times before. Olenor was scolding Lysabel for being so insensitive, and Gerrin was making the same promise he always made when his parents left. He held them both in his arms and swore that he would take care of the family until Seirrin and Nadya returned.

"I wish you were here," Gerrin said softly. "You two always knew just what to say to make everything seem so clear." He ran his thumb along the frame's edge for a moment. "I know I made a promise . . . but would you guys forgive me if I broke it?"

"Gerrin!" Eissa shouted from the top of the stairs. "Dinner's ready!"

Gerrin set his picture down on his nightstand and made his way to the dining room. Olenor, Lysabel, Eissa, and Ksara were all present and sitting at the table. They were each loading up their plates with a mix of roast beef and vegetables. The mood at the table was cheerful, something that had been scarcely seen before Ksara stumbled into town. Gerrin smiled thinking about the happenstance of the situation — that Ksara would be so hopelessly lost and that he would find her in the vastness of the desert just when he needed her most. In a way, he could say they had saved each other.

"Are you okay?" Olenor asked Gerrin. "If you stand there all night, dinner will get cold."

"I have an announcement to make," Gerrin said. "I've decided I'm going to join Ksara's crew."

Eissa squealed. She rushed over to Gerrin and wrapped her arms around him. "Promise me you'll come and visit us in Hastos sometime and tell us all about your travels."

"Of course," he replied.

"Took you long enough," Lysabel said. "I was beginning to think you might actually stay."

Ksara looked to Gerrin, and they locked eyes. "Are you sure?" she asked with a playful inflection. "Our journey will undoubtedly be filled with badassery the likes of which you have never imagined, but it will be dangerous. You could die out there."

"I can die anywhere," Gerrin replied, flashing a grin. "Might as well be with you."

Ksara returned Gerrin's gesture.. "All right," she exclaimed as she picked up her fork. "Then let us eat. Somebody pass me the meat!"

Dinner was incredible, and knowing it would be the last time he had his grandmother's cooking for a while, Gerrin made sure to savor every bite. Even so, he excused himself once he was done eating. There wasn't much he had to pack. After all, he was a man of few possessions. He debated taking his beloved picture with him for a while but decided it would be best if he left the photo for his sisters to keep.

"Knock, knock," Olenor said, descending the stairs into the basement.

"Hey Gram. I'll be back up in just a minute. I'm just making sure I'll be ready to go when Ksara is."

"I know. That's why I'm here. I have something for you."

Gerrin turned to face his grandmother. She was holding a black metal case. It reflected the light with a radiant sheen.

"Or should I say your parents have something for you," she continued.

"What's this?"

"Your parents gave this box to me the night before they left for the last time." Olenor's tone was somber, as she stared at the case. "They told me to hold onto it and give it to you when you finally left home. I haven't opened it. It never seemed right to take a peek before you did, especially after what happened to Seirrin and Nadya."

Gerrin took the case. Goosebumps coated the skin on his arms. He looked down at the box and contemplated what its contents could be. Could it be a message? A recording would mean the world to Gerrin. To hear his parent's voices again after missing them for so long. Or what if it was an heirloom? An artifact of the family entrusted to him. The possibilities were endless, and while the case filled Gerrin with anxious joy, he also felt a deep melancholy. After all, this box contained the last gift he would receive from his beloved parents.

"Well?" Olenor asked, bringing the train running through Gerrin's mind to a screeching halt. "Are you going to open it or just stand there all night?"

Gerrin took a deep breath and opened the case. He found two pistols, a chest holster, and a folded-up note inside. The pistols stood out among the box's contents and were identical except for their inscriptions. *Seirren* was etched into the barrel of one gun, and *Nadya* was carved into the other. They were slate gray with a metallic finish and didn't resemble a typical firearm. They didn't have a magazine and seemed relatively light in Gerrin's hand.

The holster was made of a dark brown leather. Or at least it seemed like leather. It was definitely animal skin, but it was tougher than anything Gerrin had ever seen before. It was so tough, it made Gerrin shudder to think what kind of creature the skin came from.

Gerrin picked up the note and unraveled it. Immediately, his focus rested solely on its contents. The house could shake until there was nothing left standing, but at that moment, nothing could pry Gerrin away from reading those words—the last words his parents had left him.

To our dearest Gerrin, the note read. *If you are reading this, it means we didn't come home this time. It also means you've had to grow up without us, and for that, we are truly sorry. But as we sit down to write this, it isn't with tears or a heavy heart. We know that no matter what the world brings to you, you are strong enough to overcome it. Take these with you on your journey, and remember that no matter where you go, we'll always be with you. Love, Mom and Dad.*

Gerrin sniffled and wiped his eyes before his tears had a chance to fall. Once finished, he made sure to fold the note up carefully and packed it with the rest of his belongings.

The night was surprisingly easy. He expected it to be reminiscent of his previous attempt at getting a good night's sleep, yet it was the opposite. Perhaps it was because he didn't have to worry about his family for the first time in years. Or maybe it was the fact that he stayed up entirely too late in an effort to pack in as much time with his sisters as he could. Whatever the case, as soon as Gerrin's head hit the sofa cushion, he found himself lost in a deep, impenetrable slumber.

The morning, however, was where the difficulties began. Eissa must have hugged her brother a thousand times. Lysabel tried to remain aloof, but her teary eyes betrayed her. Olenor handed Gerrin the cash she had been saving, and continually mentioned how proud she was that he was going out into the world to make something of himself. Even the village showed up to wave goodbye.

Gerrin sat down in the *Eclipse* driver's seat and placed his hand on the starter panel. The engine gave a slight rumble and then fell into a gentle hum.

"All right, vice-captain," Ksara said as she leaned back in the passenger seat. "Take us to Baradir and then on to Mithrandir."

"You got it, captain," Gerrin replied with a smile. "To Baradir."

THANK YOU!

First and foremost, I'd like express my appreciation to you for picking up my book. In the sea of content published out in the world, it truly warms my that you decided to pick up something I wrote and give it the time of day. Thank you, and I hope you enjoyed the ride!

If you'd like to share your thoughts and opinions on my story, please feel free to leave a review. Doing so is a great help not only to get my work out to more readers, but it also helps me improve by utilizing your feedback. To help make things simpler, scanning the QR code below will take you to your Amazon product review page.

WANT MORE FROM ME?

Had fun and want to keep the good times rolling? Check out some of my other works.

Fantasy:
Inassea Chronicles: The Blighted Flame

You can also join my newsletter to stay up to date with projects I'm working on, receive free goodies, and gain access to exclusive content.

https://bit.ly/papena-newsletter

PRONUNCIATION GUIDE

Characters

- Aegar (Eee-gar)
- Draec (Drayke)
- Eissa Ruu (Eee-suh Roo)
- Elpys (El-peez)
- Gerrin Ruu (Jeer-rin Roo)
- Jabal (Juh-ball)
- Ksara Sepheron (Sair-uh Se-fur-on)
- Lysable Ruu (Liz-uh-bell Roo)
- Mirya (Meer-eee-ya)
- Nadya (Nah-dee-yah)
- Nefion (Ne-fee-on)
- Nox (Noks)
- Olenor Ruu (Oh-lin-or Ruu)
- Ovisia (Oh-vee-see-uh)
- Seirrin (Seer-rin)
- Serril (Ser-rill)
- Zeph (Zeff)

Locations

- Baradir (Bah-rah-deer)
- Faelyn (Fay-lin)
- Hastos (Has-toes)
- Lasslail (Lass-lay-el)
- Mythrandir (Mith-ran-deer)
- Shyael (Shy-eel)

About the Author

P. A. Peña is an author writing adult science fiction and fantasy novels. He discovered his passion for writing as a child, however, he initially planned to be a mechanical engineer leaving writing as merely a hobby. It wasn't until he made it to college and received a push from his wife that he decided to seriously pursue his passion. Patrick currently resides in Michigan where he was born and raised. If he isn't writing, he is likely playing video games, watching anime, reading, or spending time with his wife and daughter.

For more information, visit patwritesbooks.com